ALWAYS BE MY BABY

MARY TING

CHAPTER ONE
THE BREAK UP
CAMMY

""Don't talk to me. Don't you ever talk to me." I crossed my arms tightly across my chest.

"Cammy." Lucas lightly smoothed his ash brown hair, slicked back with gel, his chest heaving. "Please. Just listen. Nothing happened."

"Bull. Shit." My voice was lethal calm. I braced myself against the wall to keep from dropping to the floor. "I saw you kissing that..." My lips twisted, leaving a bitter taste in my mouth at the disgust of what he had done. "...That girl with my own eyes. Don't..." I swore I wouldn't cry, but the threatening tears streamed down with no mercy.

I took a step to the side and bumped into the back of the sofa when he took a step forward. Noting I wouldn't let him near me, he stopped.

"Listen," he tried, his jaw working. "She kissed me first. I didn't kiss her back."

Lies, lies, lies. I glared at him, not bothering to wipe my tears. "The hell you didn't. I counted to five before you pulled away. I saw the way she flirted with you. I saw the way *you* flirted back." I glanced at the mug on the dining table a few feet to the left of me, debating whether to hurl it at him.

He didn't say anything, but his eyes showed a flicker of guilt.

"We're done." I yanked my keys and purse from the dining table, and walked out the door, slamming it behind me.

Quiet. It was so quiet in the hallway as I sprinted toward the elevator, unlike the screams of rage inside my head.

Icy fingers of agony gripped my heart. I never knew an emotion could physically hurt so much. I wanted to rip it out of my chest to make the pain go away. No, I should have ripped out Lucas's heart. I wasn't the violent type, but the thought did occur.

Lucas and I had started dating when we were juniors at New York University. We met in English class. It was almost love at first sight. We couldn't get enough of each other, but for the past few months, we'd been drifting apart, bickering over little things.

Was that some kind of sign from the universe that we shouldn't be together? Too late. Lucas had broken us apart. As I stared at the damned slow elevator, I realized I had made a mistake, a very huge, stupid one.

Turning in my new wedge sandals, I sprinted back, wiping the tears off my cheeks. I didn't want him to see me crying again. Taking the key out of my back pocket, I opened the door and entered.

Lucas stood exactly at the same spot, looking just as pathetic with his shoulders slumped. His green eyes I had once found heavenly pleaded with me and... were those tears? *Oh, no.* He was *not* going to make me feel sorry for him. I was the one in pain, not him. He was the idiot who cheated on me.

"Cammy," he said softly.

"Get out." I pointed to the open door. Too caught up in rage, I had stormed out of my own apartment.

"You need to give her some time and space, asshole."

I whirled toward the voice to see my roommate taking a sip of water at the dining table, facing her opened laptop, a textbook beside it. Her bedroom door had been closed, so I didn't know she was home. She must have come out when I took off.

"We need to talk this over. Please, Cammy. Nothing happened."

I shook my head and raised both of my hands as if that could prevent him from talking. "I can't do this right now. I need to cool down."

Knowing he wouldn't leave, I went to my bedroom. Leah would kick him out. The front door slammed, confirming Lucas had left. I didn't bother to close my door, knowing Leah would come right in.

"What happened?" Leah plopped on the bed beside me, her golden blonde hair bouncing on her shoulders. She wore low-rise jeans and a pink and white plaid shirt over a white, midriff-baring top.

I grabbed a tissue from my bedside table and blew junk out of my nose as tears continued to fall. After I managed to calm my breathing, I hugged my throw pillow like a teddy bear.

"I went to that stupid party for Lucas's fraternity. I was about an hour late because of my night class. He knew I was going to be late. I decided to leave class early and found him kissing that redhead. I was too shocked to move, so I stood there like an idiot and watched their make out session. I couldn't believe my eyes. The second Lucas saw me, I ran."

Leah's mouth dropped and her hazel eyes grew bigger. "You mean the same redhead you told me about last week? The one who couldn't keep her paws off Lucas?"

I heaved a breath. "Yes."

"Oh, Cammy. I'm so sorry, redhead or no." She wrapped her arms around me.

I leaned into her shoulder and closed my eyes, hoping the tears would stop, but my heart... the dagger kept digging deeper as the reality of our relationship hit me, really hit me. Lucas and I—we were over.

Sure, we could talk about what happened. But why? I would never be able to erase the image of them kissing from my mind. How could I ever trust him again? The thought of him locking lips with hers and touching me after he made out with her gave me a horrid taste in my mouth. I didn't even want him in the same room as me.

"What are you going to do?" Leah continued, her voice gentle.

"Over time I might be able to forgive him, but I will never be able to forget." A soft cry seeped out of me. "I can't believe he kissed her back. I can't believe he cheated on me." I sucked in air and bawled into my palms.

Leah caressed my arm. "Well, it's his loss. I don't mean to sound insensitive, but he's not the one for you. It's better to know now than later. My sister's best friend got dumped on her wedding night. She fell into depression, and she was a mess for a couple months. Later, she found the love of her life. I promise, someone who was meant for you will come along. Maybe not tomorrow, but soon. You just wait and see."

I believed in fate, but it was extremely difficult in my state of mind. "I know," was all I could say.

"Let's have girls' night out as soon as we can all get together. Midterms are coming up, so not sure when, but I'll call Tiffany, Julie, Vanessa, and Valerie. Okay?"

I nodded because I had nothing to say. I didn't know if I could even make the effort to get out of the house except for going to my classes.

CHAPTER TWO
GUILT
LUCAS

There were no words I could say to make it right. Guilt slammed into me again as I tried to cover the truth of what I had done. Caroline really had kissed me, but I didn't stop her. I freakin' didn't stop her, and I couldn't understand why. Cammy and I had been going out for a year, and I really loved her. *What the hell is wrong with me?*

I could have blamed it on the alcohol, but I wasn't anywhere near being buzzed. Caroline had been flirty, but she never aggressively came on to me. Cammy had warned me about Caroline more than once. She said it bothered her that Caroline and I were friends but Caroline had never tried to be friends with her. Though Cammy did attempt to make an effort to get to know Caroline. That didn't go so well.

Caroline was not only a pledge from our sister sorority but my little sis as well. So in a way, I felt obligated to do things with her and get to know her better. I'd thought Cammy was jealous without a real reason, but after what had happened, I couldn't say she was making things up.

"All better between you and Cammy?" Paul asked when I walked into my apartment and slammed the front door shut. He was getting a drink out of the fridge.

I stood there gripping my hair and heaving deep breaths.

"Ouch. That good, huh?"

"You left the party early?" I grabbed a beer out of the fridge and plopped on the sofa.

Paul sat next to me. "I'm too old to stay late. Besides, we'll both be graduating soon, and I should spend my time doing something productive."

I popped the can open and took a sip. "You're going to Harvard Graduate School. I think you can waste a little time partying."

He shrugged and took a gulp before he spoke. "So what happened? She refused to hear your side of the story?"

I took another sip, wishing I could start the night over. "She said she saw us flirting and that I kissed Caroline back," I muttered. I felt guilty for hurting Cammy. "She didn't want to talk to me. She wants time, and I don't blame her."

"What did you say after that?"

"I..." I shook my head. "I don't remember. I just left. Even if I got down on my knees and begged, she would have kicked me out. In fact, I don't remember much about the rest of the night, either. It all happened so fast, even the kiss with Caroline, which didn't freakin' mean anything. I think I was too surprised to push her away." I ran my hand down my face and blew out a long breath. "Cammy hates me. She's never going to forgive me. This is my fault. I should have stopped Caroline. I guess I was too friendly with her and she got the wrong message. Plus she drank too much. I told her friend to keep an eye out for her before I took off to find Cammy."

Paul stretched his legs and crossed his ankles on the table. "If you want to get Cammy back, I suggest you do it quickly. I know she told you she wants time, but that will only pull you two apart even more. Just talking from experience."

I angled my eyebrows. Paul had been my roommate for almost two years, since we moved out of the dorm at the end of our freshman year. We rushed fraternity together at the beginning of our junior year and had been friends ever since then. I met Cammy then. She wasn't interested in joining a sorority, but she was at one of the open parties supporting her friend Vanessa.

I'd seen Paul regularly with one girl freshman year. They must have broken up. He dated a few here and there after that, but nothing serious. And we'd never talked about his relationship since it happened before I met him.

"You're talking from experience, huh? What happened?" I thought hearing his story would give me hope that I could fix what I had broken.

He released a long sigh and took a moment before he spoke. "To make a long story short, I would have given her a second chance had she asked for it. I loved her that much, or at least I thought I was in love." He shifted to face me, his beer can dented on the side from pressing hard. "If you truly love her, then fight for her. Beg her for a second chance. Do everything you can, even if it means to tell your little sis to stay the freakin' hell away from you. Cammy is never going to trust Caroline ever again. If you want Cammy back, you've just lost your little sis. But if you don't love her, or if you're not sure, then this would be a good time to break things off."

I considered his advice.

"You're going off to graduate school this summer to get your MBA in Los Angeles. How about Cammy? She's staying here in New York, right?" He didn't give me time to answer and continued, "Have you two talked about the long-distance relationship? It's time to grow up, my friend." He patted my back and stood up. "It's late. Get some sleep."

"Yeah, thanks," I said.

There was no doubt in my mind I loved Cammy and I would do anything for her, even if it meant I would have to cut my friendship with Caroline, but Paul was right. Cammy and I had to have that talk soon, if she gave me a second chance. We'd both received our acceptance letters recently and we both put off talking about it.

I had always planned to move back home, but what about Cammy? Knowing there was no way in hell I could fall asleep, I called a few of the pledges to give them a task. Cammy didn't want to see me, but that didn't mean I couldn't do anything about it indirectly.

I needed my girl to forgive me, and I had to find a way to get her back.

CHAPTER THREE
NOT ENOUGH
CAMMY

The next morning, I dragged myself out of bed. My body ached as if I had trained for a marathon, and my heart... I wasn't sure I had one anymore. I felt nothing. Somehow, I felt disoriented from reality and time. But I had responsibilities, the only reason I forced myself out of bed.

There was no way in hell I was going to let Lucas see me with puffy eyes, if he even dared to show up at my apartment again. I'd shoved two spoons in the freezer last night, so I wrapped them in paper towels and placed them over my eyes this morning. Those darn things were so cold, I couldn't leave them on for long.

I allowed five minutes before I dashed out the door, my hair tied back into a ponytail with a scrunchie and no makeup on. The frozen spoons had alleviated the puffiness somewhat but not entirely. It would have to do.

I had been late to my job several times, no thanks to Lucas who had slept over often, and I couldn't afford to be late again. I quickly shut out the thought of Lucas and sprinted across the street to the food court where I'd worked for the last year.

"Hey, Gus." I waved and rushed to the cash register. Not only did I not want to be there, I didn't want to talk to anyone.

"You're late." He frowned, adjusting the stainless-steel containers lined up.

I gave him a small, innocent smile, not really giving a shit what he thought. He had replaced Stacey, the other manager whom I adored. Even though it had been a month, I still missed her. A Backstreet Boys song was playing, and I lost myself in the music.

"Uh, what?" I mouthed the words to the song.

"You're late," he repeated, with a sting in his voice.

"Sorry. I'm only late five minutes and we just opened. Besides, nobody comes to the burrito station for breakfast." I gestured toward the bakery shop across from us. They sold muffins and coffee and all kinds of yummy stuff. As if on cue, as if God played a trick on me, a couple lined up to order.

Gus smirked, but his eyes fell down to my bare legs and my gray penny loafers. *Pervert. Or maybe he liked my shoes.* I usually didn't wear shorts to work, but what the hell. It wasn't like I was working in a professional office.

As lunchtime approached, the line became longer. Tracy, who worked only for three hours every day for lunch, finally arrived. She too was five minutes late. I narrowed my eyes at Gus, who simply rolled his eyes as if to say, yes, I know she's late and don't you dare say anything to me.

"Hey, Cammy." Tracy smiled and went to help Gus. She sported Calvin Klein jeans and jelly platform shoes. A black plastic choker necklace hugged her neck. Not one I would wear, but it looked cute on her.

I smiled in reply with a wave of my hand. We worked fast and diligently, moving the line, but even then the time seemed to creep by. My body weighed a ton. Every step was a struggle, and every word was an effort.

I ducked lower from embarrassment when I spotted a few of Lucas's fraternity pledges. They had been at the party and no doubt saw what had happened. Ugh! I wish I could disappear, better yet, make them disappear.

Crap! They filed in line.

"Six forty-eight," I said to the girl in front of me, holding a tray of Gus's special burrito and a soft drink.

She dug into her wallet and pulled out a five and a dollar. "Shoot. This is all I have. Can you just skip the drink?"

"Let me see..." I reached inside my front pocket, recalling I had shoved some change in the last time I wore those shorts. "Ah." I pulled out two quarters. "I've got you covered."

She lifted a corner of her mouth. "You're so sweet. Thank you for covering for me. I promise to pay you back."

"Whatever. It's small change." I moved on to the next person after giving her a smile.

Then...

The scent of warm spices and rich, dark wood filled my nostrils. Beautiful, crystal-blue eyes met mine under a mop of brown hair turned molten gold under the sunlight pouring from the glass ceiling. I tried not to stare, but for a brief moment, he made me forget about Lucas.

I dropped my eyes to his plate, feeling guilty. But then I thought better and reminded myself I was allowed to admire a good-looking guy. My hands were to myself and... Lucas cheated on me.

"You got a burrito, a taco, and a drink." I tapped on the register. "That'll be eight."

He handed me a twenty, and gorgeous dimples pierced his cheeks. "Cammy."

I blinked, taking a few seconds to register. I had never seen him before, or maybe I'd never paid attention to other guys ever since Lucas and I had been a couple.

"How do you know my name?" I asked, handing him back his change. His hand felt warm when I accidentally brushed it.

When he let out a soft chuckle, his broad and thick chest bobbed a bit. What was so funny?

He cleared his throat and pointed at my name tag.

I flushed with warmth and let out a snort. "Oh. That. Of course." *Stupid me.*

"Anyway, you're in my economics class. A group of us are studying for the midterm tomorrow night. Would you like to join us?"

He noticed me in that lecture room? Impressive.

"I don't know." I chewed the inside of my mouth.

For the past year, I'd avoided group study, especially when getting an invite from a guy. We had fought about it one time. Lucas told me the guy had only asked me so he could move in on me. Since it bothered him so much, I declined all the group studies. Now that the leash was severed...

"Please join us if you can." He lowered his bottom lip and gave me puppy dog eyes.

Oh. My. God. I would have said yes to anything he asked with that pout, but I restrained myself.

"We're meeting at the library at seven," he continued. "I promise to behave. And by the way, my name is Grayson." He winked and left.

I stared at his cool swagger, his jeans and T-shirt molding so nicely to his body. Girls from nearby tables watched him walk out the door. And I was thinking of Lucas again. Why the hell was I feeling guilty for lusting over a guy's body? Lucas kissed Caroline, I reminded myself again.

"I don't blame you. He's so fine. So yummy. Say yes, or I'll attend the group study for you."

I spun to Gus, practically breathing down my neck, drooling was more like it. I had wondered about Gus, but that removed my uncertainty about his romantic preferences.

"By the way, I love your shorts with those shoes," he added, checking out my ass.

I patted the rhinestones adorning the back pockets thinking it all made sense. "Thanks. I love them, too."

Gus went back to attending the customers, and a frown replaced my smile when Lucas's fraternity pledges gave me a knowing grin. I gasped when the three of them got down on their knees and started to sing loud and clear.

I'm sorry Cammy. For hurting you. You are the love of my life. I'm such a fool. Please take me back. For I love you still. My heart dies a little bit more every second we are apart. I can't breathe without you. I can't live without you. I'll make it up to you. You'll always be my baby. This I promise you.

They stood up, bowed, and one of the guys handed me a dozen beautiful red roses I had not seen him holding. Everyone in the food court clapped, the sound echoing like raindrops. Before I could protest, the bouquet was in my hands and they had left.

Tears burned my eyes, but I held them back, reminding myself I was at work. Lucas could be sweet and romantic, but it had been a very long time since he paid attention to me like that. I knew he was sorry, but my heart had already shattered. It was going to take time.

"They're beautiful," Tracy cooed behind me. "He hurt you that bad? What did he do?"

Tracy was new to the job and a freshman, and she needed to learn to shut her mouth. I didn't say anything.

Gus shook his head with sad eyes. I didn't need his sympathy.

Great! Now the whole world knew Lucas and I had a fight. Lucas's sweet gesture of apology did tug my heart. A part of me wanted to forgive him and take him back, but I couldn't help seeing the image of them kissing.

I had warned Lucas about Caroline *so* many times. He brushed it off and told me I was "just jealous." The roses and the stupid song would not make the pain go away. I cursed him under my breath, tossed the roses in the trash, and got back to work.

Gus gawked at me, and Tracy almost fetched back the roses but stopped when I gave her the evil eye.

CHAPTER FOUR
UNFORGIVABLE
CAMMY

"He didn't." Leah parted her mouth in shock and then passed me a plate of salad.

I shrugged as if it were no big deal. "He wrote a stupid apology song." I gritted my teeth. "As if."

Leah's expression softened and so did her hazel eyes. "Well, I have to give him some credit for trying." She speared a fork through a bite of chicken in her salad, shoved it in her mouth, and spoke again. "You could have brought the roses home. They would have made our apartment smell nice."

I cringed. "I know. They were so pretty, but I was so mad." My fingers tightened on my fork. "Does he think he could make me forget what he did that easily?"

Leah took a sip of water. "I don't know. But he's trying. Not that I'm on his side. What he did was unforgivable."

I released a breath and bit into a crouton. "I know I sound like a broken record, but if he found me kissing another guy, he would go apeshit."

Leah waved her fork at me. "But the point is he would never have found you kissing another guy, Cammy. You wouldn't have cheated on him. You don't even notice other males around you."

I didn't say anything. Still pissed off at Lucas, I just shoved more lettuce into my mouth and chewed like a horse.

"I don't mean to sound insensitive, but..." She examined me carefully. "Isn't Lucas moving back home after we graduate? He got accepted to the USC MBA program, right? And you're staying in New York, right?" She knitted her eyebrows together, silently answering her questions before I had the chance to speak. "So maybe it's better this way. I mean, not the part of him cheating, but if you can't trust him when he's in New York with you, how are you going to trust him when he's in LA? Perhaps you two are not meant to be together."

I nodded, gnawing the inside of my mouth. Leah was right. "Lucas and I need to talk things through. We hadn't had a chance to talk about the future. We just found out, and we kind of ignored the issue. I need a couple more days to let the steam settle. I don't know what I'm going to do."

"I understand." Leah stabbed the edamame beans with her fork. "I was in the same boat as you. It was the reason why John and I decided to break up. The distance was too much for us. I found out he's seeing someone and I'm happy for him."

"I remember," I reminded her. It was one of the darkest times for Leah. It just happened last year, but she talked about it as if it happened many years ago.

"We need to talk about what's going to happen after we graduate, too."

I chewed and swallowed. "Since I got accepted to NYU, I'm going to continue to live with you. I'm not planning to move back home."

She released a soft sigh of relief. "Good."

"What are you going to do?" I picked up a small slice of sourdough bread and buttered it.

"I'm going to keep working as an administrative assistant for the law firm and see where that takes me for now, but don't worry, I'll be your roommate. You'll miss me too much if I leave." She flashed an innocent smile with a wink.

"Of course I will. You better not leave me. You've been like a sister to me for the past three years."

"I know. You need me too much." She giggled.

Though my heart was still filled with stones, eating with Leah and talking about what had happened and about our future made me feel a little bit better—just a tiny little bit.

CHAPTER FIVE
MAMA'S BEAR
LUCAS

"What?" I clenched my jaw while I gripped the doorframe. It took every ounce of my willpower not to punch the wall. "What the hell do you mean she threw the roses in the trash? Are you sure?"

Greg, the pledge that gave her the roses said with a calm voice, "I handed the roses to her after we sang the song just like you said. I snuck back in after we walked out. I saw her chuck them in the trash behind her."

My fists rounded, tightening 'til my knuckles ached. "Those roses weren't cheap. I can't believe she just trashed them like it meant nothing to her." I swallowed, realizing I was talking to a pledge I barely knew. "Sorry. Thanks for your help. I'll make sure you get points for helping an active."

Greg nodded and left. When I shut the door, Paul came out of his bedroom.

"I'm going to chill out at Mama's Bear. Do you want to go?" Paul asked.

"Cammy hates me." I raked my hair back with a huff. "She tossed the roses I gave her in the trash, man. Who does that?"

Paul gently pushed me toward the door. "You need a drink, and I'm starving. Let's talk in the car."

It only took us about ten minutes to get to Mama's Bear, so we didn't talk much, but I was able to tell him what I had done, about the song and roses.

The restaurant was packed, mostly with our fraternity brothers and our sister sorority. Great. Caroline would most likely be there. I needed to talk to her anyway. Now was as good a time as any, I supposed.

It had been a long time since I showed up on a Friday night. Cammy and I would go out to dinner or we would have a private night at either of our places. It felt strange to be there without her. My heart sank at the thought of Cammy and what I had done or, rather, what I had failed to do.

"Hey," I said to the guys and peeps sitting at the long rectangular tables that sat about thirty or more as a song from the Smashing Pumpkins blasted.

After Paul and I made our rounds of greeting, we sat by the bar. I came so I wouldn't be alone at home to think about Cammy and also to keep Paul company. After we ordered dinner, the bartender gave us our drinks. I kept checking my black pager hoping Cammy would page me.

"Hey, Paul. Lucas."

I stiffened and placed my mug down. Caroline and two of her friends were smiling when I turned to the voice.

"I didn't know you were coming." Caroline tried to sound casual, but I got a hint of nervousness in her tone.

"I'll be right back," I said to Paul and grabbed Caroline with me to go to the back.

"What's going on?" She bored her eyes into mine, her facial muscles tightening.

"We need to talk." I narrowed my eyes at her. "You shouldn't have kissed me. Now you've ruined our friendship and the brother and sister thing." I pointed between her and me.

She bit her bottom lip and her eyes hardened. "It was just a kiss. It didn't mean anything. Why, did Cammy tell you not to be my big bro? That's not possible."

You broke Cammy and me up, I wanted to say, but I didn't want to give her the satisfaction.

She took a step toward me and stabbed me with her index finger. "It's all your fault. You were flirting with me. So maybe I took that as an invitation. Besides, you kissed me first."

I shoved my fingers through my hair, trying to calm the anger. "I don't remember what happened. I only remembered you kissed me and I was in shock."

"No, you do remember," she said almost too seductively, caressing both of my arms.

I pushed her arms away, took a step back, and growled, "Don't touch me. I don't care about the damned rules. You're not my little sis anymore. Don't call me. Don't talk to me." With that, I walked away, back to Paul.

"What happened?" he asked over the music that seemed to have gotten louder.

"I'll tell you later. Let's just eat and go. I can't stand this anymore. I'm going to Cammy's place tomorrow to get this straightened out."

"Fine with me." He glanced toward a table of girls obnoxiously singing *Waterfalls* by TLC and then back to me. "I'm too old for this crowd and the music is too loud."

"We're only twenty-one, but your oldness is rubbing off on me." I snorted.

The waitress placed our plates of hamburgers and fries in front of us. Paul's eyes lingered on the waitress as she walked away. I dared not look, thinking of Cammy.

CHAPTER SIX
THE GROUP STUDY
CAMMY

"Are you sure you're going to be fine?" I checked to make sure Leah had everything she needed. Water, medicine, a plastic bag to throw up in, her pager, and the phone close to her.

"I'm not a child, Cammy. I'll be fine. Go to your group study," she said wearily with her eyes closed. "I'm just going to sleep."

"But you have the flu, Leah." I raised the blanket a bit higher, past her arm. Even wearing sweats, she shivered.

Leah glanced at the bedside table with one eye peeled slightly open. "I have everything I need. You're such a good friend. Now go. Who's in your group? Do I know anyone in your group?"

"No. I don't think so."

I suddenly felt guilty. I wouldn't be going to this group study if a hot guy hadn't asked me to join. He was only being nice, I told myself.

Nothing was going on. Besides, it wasn't going to be just the two of us.

"Well," I continued, my voice rising, "this guy from my economics class asked me to join his group."

"Oh really?" Despite her fever, Leah giggled. "Does this guy have a name?"

"Grayson Parker."

"Grayson Parker?" She sounded like she either knew him or found his name to be strange. "Does he have blue eyes, light brownish air, a very hot body, and is a bit taller than six feet?"

"Yes," I drawled. "Do you know him?"

Leah flashed her eyes open and sat up. Her hair stuck out and makeup was smeared under her eyes. "He's Grayson. All the single and not-single girls are drooling after him. I know a few girls who have asked him out, and he declined. We thought he had a girlfriend. But oh my God, Cammy. He asked you out?"

"No." My face paled. Was that guilt? Did he ask me out? Did I say yes? "No," I said again. "I— He … he asked me to join a study group."

Leah at last surrendered and fell back to her pillow with her eyes closed. "Have fun."

I closed the door, grabbed my backpack, and strolled to the library. Peace and quiet pervaded the room. Most of the seats were taken. The sound of shoes clicking and pages flipping filled the air.

I went through double doors and searched for Grayson. Besides Grayson, I had no idea who else was in our group. Maybe this was a bad idea. Just as I decided to go back home, soft air brushed against my ear, and that warm, spicy scent filled me.

"Looking for me, Cammy?" a low, manly voice whispered, producing shivers through me.

I whirled, gulping down air. My heart thumped faster as my eyes set on his heavenly blue ones. So blue, gazing into them felt like floating in a cloudless sky. He wore jeans, a flannel, and a baseball cap backward.

"Huh. Hey." I suddenly forgot his name. I forgot how to breathe. I forgot who and where I was.

"Good. 'Cause I've been looking for you, too, and now I've found you. I realized I forgot to tell you which table. I didn't have your phone number. I couldn't call you. We need to fix that problem right now." He took out a piece of paper from his back pocket. "Do you have a beeper?"

I nodded.

"Your phone and pager number please." After I told him, he gave me a little notepaper with his number on it. "Now you have both of mine, too. This way." Placing a gentle hand behind my back, he took me to the table next to the tall bookcase.

Two girls and two guys sat at a round table. They smiled when they saw us approach. Thank God they were friendly and welcoming. After Grayson introduced us, we got right down to business. Two hours later, we were done and out the door. We had a great review session, and I felt ready to take the test.

"This was great, Grayson. Thank you for inviting me." I shivered as the night breeze suddenly became cooler. Spring wind was unpredictable.

Before I could blink, Grayson took off his long-sleeve, red and black flannel shirt and draped it over me. He wore a black T-shirt underneath. My treacherous eyes darted to his hard biceps when they curved around me. I dipped my chin lower.

"Oh. Thank you. Anyway, I should get going." I adjusted my backpack and veered away.

"Let me walk you home." He slid right next to me.

"You don't have to. I just live across the street." I quickened my steps.

"It's dark and it's late. I'd feel better if I walked you back. I'm doing this more for me than you, you know." He gave me a sly grin, those adorable dimples deepening.

I snorted. "Fine. But you've been warned, I'm a jaywalker or whatever you call it."

He chuckled.

After we passed through the parking lot and through a few low bushes, we stopped at the curb. I scanned both ways and before I could tell him to run, he grabbed my hand and burst out, "Run."

I didn't pull my hand away but kept running and let him guide me. We halted to catch our breath, and just then a cop car passed by. We exchanged glances and raised our eyebrows.

"That was too close," I said. "Getting a ticket for jaywalking would be too embarrassing."

"I hear ya," he agreed as he continued to follow me. "But that was fun. It's like playing Frogger."

"I played that when I was a kid, too." I smiled.

After crossing through mid-thigh high bushes, a parking lot appeared and then finally my apartment.

"Well. This is my stop. Thank you for walking me, even though you didn't have to." I took out my key from my back pocket and dangled it. "I would invite you in for a drink or something..." *God, did I just say those words? Say something unpretentious.* "I mean, you know, to thank you for inviting me, but my roommate isn't feeling well. She has a fever."

Grayson frowned and adjusted his cap. "Does she need medicine, or do you need anything?"

So sweet. Why does he have to be so sweet?

"We have everything we need. But thank you. And thank you again for asking me. The study group helped."

He nodded and shoved his hands in his jean pockets. "I'm glad you agreed to come and actually came." He grinned. I couldn't stop staring at his dimples. "By the way, if you get a one - one from me on your pager, it means hello. So, I'll see you in class tomorrow. Good luck on your test."

"You too." I handed his flannel shirt back. With a smile, I entered my apartment and closed the door behind me.

Guilt poured into me. I shoved Lucas aside. It wasn't a date, I reminded myself. I didn't cheat. But I couldn't understand the butterflies fluttering inside my gut.

Was I falling out of love with Lucas? And maybe he was falling out of love with me? Possibly the reason for our frequent fights lately?

I tiptoed to check up on Leah. When I placed my hand on her forehead, she grabbed my hand. I yelped and jumped back.

"Oh my God, you scared me." I pressed a hand on my chest.

"The medicine kicked in, I feel much better. I'm just tired," she said softly.

I placed a bottle of water with a straw inside it next to her lips. "Drink."

She shifted sideways and started sipping. "Thanks, Mom." Leaning back, she asked, "So, how was Mr. Hot Guy?"

I put the water bottle on the night table and playfully glared at her. "Mr. Hot Guy is just a friend. There were four other people with us. It wasn't a date."

"Uh huh." Her lips perked. "He's so sweet and has the cutest dimples."

I crossed my arms and scowled. "If you like him that much, then you should go out with him."

"He didn't ask me out. He asked you." She closed her eyes and waved a hand. "He has your number, doesn't he?"

I recalled when he asked for it. "Yes, and pager number. It doesn't mean anything."

The doorbell chimed.

"Maybe it's him again," she cooed.

"Shut up." I rolled my eyes.

The doorbell chimed again.

I dismissed her words and headed for the door, but a little tiny part of me wished what she said came true. Stupid me forgot to check the peephole and opened the door.

CHAPTER SEVEN
JEALOUSY
LUCAS

I couldn't take it anymore. Missing the hell out of Cammy, I needed to see her. Paul was right. The more time I gave her, the harder it would be to patch up my mistake. She needed to know I would have nothing to do with Caroline, that I would pick her over anyone.

I didn't bother to page her or call, knowing she wouldn't answer the phone. So when I stopped by her place, no one seemed to be home, even though a faint light glowed through the blinds. No one answered when I knocked on the door. It was after midnight.

Where the hell is she? Out with her friends on Saturday night? Possibly.

I went back to my car and decided to come tomorrow morning when I spotted Cammy with another guy.

My heart sank to my stomach and the world spun out of control. Calm down, I told myself. Old friends? Cammy didn't have any guy friends that I knew of.

When he leaned closer, she didn't move away. It took every ounce of my willpower not to go over there and punch his face. She smiled at him the way she smiled at me when we first started dating.

I searched deep in my memory of the past few months. Cammy and I had been fighting more than before. It was mostly over Caroline, but maybe she was trying to find an excuse to break up with me and date that guy?

He didn't kiss her, but still I couldn't wrap my mind around what I saw. After Cammy went inside, the guy took off. I debated whether to confront him. But why? I didn't know what was going on, and I certainly didn't want to look like an ass or make a fool of myself. Enough was enough.

I pressed the doorbell, and a few seconds later, I did again. Be patient, I chided myself. I waited and waited... the longer I waited, the harder my heart thundered against my rib cage. *What if she never wants to see me again?*

The door swung open. Her smile faded. She looked absolutely amazing in her cutoff jeans, crop top, and her blonde hair in a scrunchie. And those gorgeous amber eyes I'd missed so much nearly had me kneeling on the floor, begging her to take me back.

"Lucas?" She sounded off guard, in shock.

Was she expecting that guy?

"Cammy," I said softly. "Can we please talk?"

I braced myself for the door to slam in my face, but she nodded and opened it wider. "Come in. Do you want anything to drink?"

"No." I sat on the sofa.

I wanted to wrap my arms around her, smell the sweet scent of her, and kiss her. A kiss that would tell her how sorry I was and to make up for hurting her, hurting us.

When Cammy sat on the opposite side of me, I felt the division. A sturdy wall had risen between us, and I realized then it was going to take a lot more than begging and apologizing to bring it down.

"Cammy." I reached out for her hand but dropped mine instead. I'd wanted to see her so badly that I hadn't planned a speech. *What the hell do I say?* So I poured out my heart. "I'm so sorry, baby. It's killing me that I've hurt you. You have to believe me that I'm hurting, too. I told Caroline that I never want to talk to her again. I've said this before, but she kissed me. I was in shock, and I might not have pushed her away. But I swear, baby. She means nothing to me."

A tear slid down Cammy's face. "I told you to be careful about Caroline, but you didn't listen. You let her in. I can't look at you without thinking of her lips on yours."

I scrubbed my face, releasing a deep sigh. I wasn't making any progress. "Cammy. I'm begging." I went to her and dropped my head onto her lap. She stiffened. "Please, Cammy. Give us another chance. Let's heal our wounds together. Just tell me what you want me to do. I'll do anything."

Her body trembled slightly and a soft whimpering noise escaped from her. "I need time. I can't—"

Anger rose from the pit of my gut. I sat up with my jaw clenching. "Is it because of that guy?"

Cammy wiped her cheeks, her eyes wide. "What guy?"

"I came earlier to talk to you and I saw you with that guy. Who is he?" I shouldn't have raised my tone, but too late.

Cammy got up, putting more distance between us. "It's none of your business, but he's just a friend."

"Does he know that? Did you tell him you don't have a boyfriend anymore? Are you telling me you want more time so you can decide whether you want him or me?"

Jealousy raged in me. *Why can't she give me a second chance? I get that she needs more time, but...*

"Get out." She pointed at the door. "For your information, he walked me to my apartment because it was late at night. We were in a study group. He was concerned for me.

Were you concerned about me when you kissed that girl in front of all your freakin' brothers? And another thing. We never talked about our future. You're moving back to LA, and I'm going to be here. Did you not have the balls to break up with me, so you had to tell me by kissing what's her face?"

"We-we didn't get a chance to talk about it," I stammered. "Maybe *you* were trying to tell me something by going behind my back and flirting with that guy." Some corner of my brain knew I made no sense, but I was beyond mad. I breathed out. "Listen, we both should act like mature adults and stop before we say something we regret."

Cammy scowled, her face as tight as ever. "Maybe you should have thought of that before you kissed that skank."

I lost it and raised my voice. "I'm sorry, Cammy. I'll say it thousands of times. She kissed me. Can you please forgive me and just move on together?"

Cammy rubbed her eyebrows with her thumb and forefinger. "If you saw me kissing a guy, could you forgive me?"

A trick question. "If he pushed himself on you like Caroline did, and you didn't kiss him back, like me..." I stressed that point. "...then, yes."

She tilted her head, her eyes unfocused, considering my answer. "I don't know a whore that would push himself on me." She smirked. "So, I get to kiss a guy. If you can handle it without freaking out, then I'll give us a chance. If you lose it, then we're done."

"What?" I nearly choked. "You're kidding, right?"

She angled her eyebrows with her arms crossed. "Would I joke about that?"

I shifted on my feet. "You're going to kiss a guy and tell me about it?"

"No," she drawled that one little word. "I'm going to kiss him in front of you."

"Cammy. That's crazy."

"Is it? I want you to feel what I felt. Then you'll know it's not so easy to wipe the image of someone kissing me out of your mind."

"Fine." I massaged the back of my neck. "When are you going to do this?" And I couldn't believe I made the most ridiculous bet with my girlfriend. Regardless of what she thought, we were still together. We hadn't officially broken up, not yet.

"I don't know." She sounded hesitant. *Perhaps she'll change her mind?*

"Fine. I can't believe we're doing this." With that, I walked out the door, angrier than I'd been before.

Kiss another guy in front of me. I can handle it.

Whatever it would take to get her back.

CHAPTER EIGHT
MY ROOMMATE
CAMMY

"You did what?" Leah shrieked the next morning when I told her the bet I made with Lucas.

I handed her a mug of coffee and sat across from her on the dining table. Savoring a sip, I said, "It just happened. I was so pissed off at him that I just said it. He thinks it's so easy for me to take him back after he kissed that girl. How could he think I could just forget it like it never happened?"

"I don't know, but I have to say, you're sneaky." She covered her hands around the mug, taking in the warmth.

"Sneaky?"

"Well, sneaky might not be the word, but are you going to kiss Grayson?" She eyed me carefully.

I almost spit out my tea I had just drunk. "No. Why would you say that? I mean, I think he's very attractive, but I don't have thoughts of him like that. Though I told Lucas any guy. I should kiss someone he dislikes as much as I hate that girl. I can't even say her name. I should kiss a guy from the other frat. That would piss him off." Then I thought about what I had said. "I'm being ridiculous, aren't I? I'm acting so immature about this. This isn't me."

Leah perked her pretty pink lips and shook her head. Then her hazel eyes beamed. "But I like the new you. Cunning. Evil. And he deserves it. I've told you so many times he's not good enough for you. He doesn't treat you like you deserve. You're one in a million, Cammy. He took that for granted. It's his freakin' fault for being stupid enough to let a freshman bitch get in the way of your relationship."

I shook my head. "I don't know, Leah. This isn't who I am. I don't think I'll have the guts to kiss a stranger, to use him like that."

"Then kiss a guy you know. Tell him your plan, no strings attached. And I bet this guy will be more than willing to kiss you. You tell Lucas where and when. Then just do it. Kiss and it's over."

"You make it sound so simple," I groaned then savored another sip. "The problem is, I don't know any guys. I mean, I know lots of guys, but most of them know Lucas and they would never do what I ask."

Leah twitched her eyebrows, giving me a mischievous smile. "You know Grayson."

My cheeks warmed. "I can't. I barely know him. And besides, I need to be in his study group. It was the best study group I've ever attended, not that I've been to many, but it was helpful."

Leah leaned back into the chair, her fingers still hugging the mug. "How can you compare? In all three years I've known you, you've only been to two group studies. That's not much to compare, Cammy. So don't make up any excuses. Besides, who else can you ask?"

I shook my head. "I made a stupid bet out of anger. One of us is going to get burned."

"It ain't going to be you, sista." Leah gazed at me under those long eyelashes. Lucky for her, she didn't have to use mascara.

I tapped on my mug. "Honestly, I don't think I can go through with this."

"I won't tell you what to do Cammy, but either do this and get it out of your system, or take Lucas back or dump him. Make a decision."

"How do you leave someone you love? I still love him. I'm just so angry at what he did. He's truly sorry. I know he is."

"I understand. This is your first real relationship. The first break up is very difficult. But if Lucas isn't the one, you have to let him go. I want you to find the kind of love you can't let go. And if you can see yourself without him, then it's over. Don't try to mend what is already broken and unrepairable."

My fingers slowly traced the rim of the empty mug. "You're right. I still don't know what I'm going to do, but you're right."

She waved a hand. "Just let it happen or sleep on it. That's what I always do."

"The reason you're always relaxed and the reason I'm stressed as hell."

Leah giggled. "When you've been through hell and back plenty of times, you learn to laugh about it. It's all good. Anyway, your mom called and left a message on the answering machine."

"Thank you. I mean for everything."

Leah reached over and rested her hand on mine. "Anytime. You're my nurse and I'm your therapist."

We shared a laugh.

"You working today?" She finished her coffee with a long gulp.

"It's Sunday, remember?"

"Fever can do funny things to your brain." She snorted. "Well, I don't feel like studying, and I don't want to be indoors. Let's go shopping."

"Are you okay to be out? I mean you just got over a fever."

Leah stood up and took my empty mug. "Don't be my nurse right now. We both need some sun, Snow White."

I glanced down at my arm and then to Leah's smooth, golden brown skin. *Lucky.*

"Fine," I snapped playfully with a flip of my messy blonde hair.

CHAPTER NINE
THE PHONE CALL
CAMMY

Leah and I had a blast shopping. We spent three hours at the mall, grabbed something light to eat for dinner, and then finally came home. After I washed and plopped into bed, I called my mom.

"Cammy. How are you?"

"Good. How are you?"

"I'm calling because I haven't heard from you."

"Sorry. I've been very busy. It's only been a week, Mom."

I sounded a bit sassy, so I paused to change my tone. After my fight with Lucas, I hadn't felt like talking to even my mom or my sister.

"I know, but I was getting used to you calling me every other day."

"Sorry, Mom. How're Casey and Peter?"

After my parents divorced, my mom married Peter when I was in high school. I rarely spoke to my father, especially since he moved back to London. I visited him last summer, but with the time change, it was difficult to call, not to mention how expensive it was to call overseas.

"They're fine. Casey isn't home right now. She got a job at the bakery, and she's making her own graduation cards. She got accepted to the culinary school she wanted to attend in San Francisco."

I shifted on my bed and coiled the telephone cord around my finger. "She did? Great for her. I can't believe my little sister is graduating from high school in three months."

"You'll be there, won't you?" Not a question, but not a demand.

"Of course. I only have one sister, and you guys are only an hour away."

"Good."

"Give Peter my love."

"He's right next to me."

"He's not working in the ER today?"

Mom met Peter at the Emergency Care in the county hospital, where she was a nurse. They were friends to lovers. He had been there for her through a rough marriage and divorce, and they discovered they wanted to be more than friends.

"Nope. He got the day off." Mom sounded excited.

"Well, enjoy your time together, and I'll swing by home next Sunday."

"How's Lucas?"

I tried to hang up the phone before she could ask, since she always asked about him on every phone conversation we had, but too late.

I told her half a truth. "He's fine. I saw him yesterday."

"He's welcome to come over next Sunday. Let me know and I'll cook a homemade meal."

Her words squeezed my heart. And I couldn't find the words to tell her what had happened. Before my tears could fall, I said, "Mom I have to go. I'll talk to you soon. Love you." Then I hung up.

I tried not to think of Lucas, and spending most of the day with Leah helped, but I had to face reality. Lying in my bed — safe and warm — in the comfort of my own making, took me away from life. And that stupid bet. I had made it out of spite. Ugh! I didn't want to think about it. I would let it happen or sleep on it. That was what Leah had told me to do.

Just as I was about to drift away to the serene calm of sleep, the phone rang. Thinking it might be Lucas, I decided to let the answering machine do it instead, but then I remembered Leah was staying up late to study for her mid-term.

"Cammy, it's for you," Leah shouted through my door, but she said it with a hint of playfulness I had never heard her use just to tell me to pick up the phone.

"Thanks." I answered, "Hello."

I heard the click from Leah.

"Cammy. It's me, Grayson."

My eyes shot open, and I bolted up. "Grayson?" My tone rose. "Grayson," I tried again, that time achieving a neutral tone. "Hi. What's up? I mean did you need something?" Geez. I sounded nervous.

"No. I thought I'd call and see if you had any questions or if you wanted to ask questions or if you just wanted to talk." He was rambling, too. "Because the test is tomorrow." A light chuckle rambled through the phone. "I think I asked you the same question in three different ways."

Leah's head popped through the crack of my door with a broad smile.

I stuck out my tongue at her. "That's fine. It's so sweet of you to call, but I think I'll be fine. Like I said before, the review group was awesome and everyone was helpful. I'm ready for the test."

Leah plopped on my bed, tugging the phone so she could hear. As silly as it was, feeling like we were in high school, I let her.

"Good." A pause. "If you're free, maybe we could have lunch together after the test. My treat."

"No. I should be the one treating you." I slapped my forehead. Did I offer to not only have lunch but to pay?

"Great. Then it's a... lunch. I don't need to pick you up since we'll be in the same class."

"Uh?"

"It's just lunch," Leah whispered, lightly socking my arm. "He didn't ask you to sleep with him or kiss him, for crying out loud, Cammy."

"Okay, Grayson. I'll see you in class, and it's a lunch date. I mean—we'll have lunch—as friends." Oh dear God. Shoot me now.

After we hung up, Leah waggled her eyebrows. "Lunch date?"

"I didn't say that."

She giggled.

"Why?" I glared.

"Why what?" She played innocent, sitting up with her legs crossed.

I scooted to the headboard, pillows supporting my back. "Why do you want me to date Grayson?"

"Because..." Leah's face grew solemn. "Anyone is better than Lucas."

"Is he that bad? I mean besides the thing he did?" I didn't understand. I didn't think he was a bad boyfriend.

Leah wiggled her toes and stared at my desk as if the answers were stored there. "When you were sick with a stomach bug, what did Lucas do?"

"He bought me medicine."

"True, but did he stay? Did he get you something to eat?"

I almost said yes, but... "I don't remember. I'm hardly ever sick. He called to check up on me."

She cocked an eyebrow. "I remember. He didn't do shit. You are so sweet and kind and giving, Cammy. You don't expect much from others, yet you give one hundred percent of yourself to others. Because you know Lucas can be selfish and all about himself, you don't expect anything from him. So everything is fine. But you know what, Cammy? It's not fine. You deserve someone who will tend to your heart as you do his, if not more. You deserve someone that cares about you when you're sick. You deserve someone that walks you home. Grayson walked you home. That's why I like him for you."

"Leah." It was the first time she had spilled so much of her feelings about Lucas, and I didn't know what to say.

"Let me tell you from my own experience. There are a *lot* of guys out there." She pointed to the direction of our campus. "Most of them would love to go out with you, but only a few would treat you like a man who truly loves his woman with everything he is. And when you find someone like him, you don't let go. I believe Lucas finally figured out how awesome you are. That's why he's having difficulty letting you go. He told you he didn't kiss her back, but your own eyes do not lie. Your mind knows the truth, but your heart refuses to believe it. I know that feeling. I've been there before."

I knew Leah had a bad breakup, but it had happened during the summer. She went back home to Michigan and didn't tell me much about it. We talked about it over the phone, but she had told me she was fine. And every time the subject of her ex came up, she spoke as if they broke up on good terms. I still didn't understand the full story. Leah was private at times, so I respected her boundaries and didn't probe.

"Was it bad, Leah? Your breakup?" Perhaps she would be willing to share more since we were on the subject — sort of.

"I realized he wasn't the man I wanted forever with. He was selfish and cocky. Everything was about him. And when we got into a fight, it wasn't our fault. It became my fault. So I was the one apologizing all the time. I was tired of saying I'm sorry. To him, he was always right and never took the responsibility that perhaps he was in the wrong. Lucas reminds me a lot of my ex. I'm sorry, Cammy. I don't mean to tell you what to do. You are a grown woman. You make up your mind and you sleep on the bed you make, but I hate to see you waste your time on a guy that doesn't deserve you. I get it. He's your first serious boyfriend. But when you find the one you're supposed to be with, the one you want forever with, you'll forget about Lucas."

Confused, hurt, and angry, I soaked in everything that poured out of her heart and then sobbed in her arms.

CHAPTER TEN
BIRD POOP
CAMMY

I barely made it to class on time the next day. I'd thought I hit snooze, but instead, I accidentally shut off my alarm. Running across the street, instead of crossing at the crosswalk, reminded me of Grayson and his comment about playing Frogger.

It put a smile on my face as I ran to class, but it quickly turned to a frown when I spotted the pledges that sang to me. Out of breath, I made it in the nick of time.

"Cammy. I almost went to your apartment. Are you okay?" Grayson diverted me to the very back row. He had his backpack and a book to save our seats.

"I nearly had a heart attack." I dabbed the sweat off my forehead with the back of my hand and sank into the seat.

Grayson's eyes widened.

I gently touched his arm. It felt so natural to place my hand there. No guilt. Just friendship. "Sorry. I don't mean it literally." I snorted.

After I took out my number two pencils, I shoved my backpack under my seat just as the tests were being passed out. Sixty questions. My palms became sweaty. Taking tests, whether I studied or not, always made me nervous and panicky.

When I felt Grayson's eyes on me, I turned to him.

His cheeks pinched inward, his dimples deepened, and his stunning blue eyes beamed. "You might not want to eat that." He took the pencil out of my mouth and handed it to me. "I promise to feed you after the test."

"I-I tend to bite my pencil during tests or when I get nervous," I confessed.

His eyebrows lifted and his lips spread wickedly. Leaning closer, his shoulder touched mine and his leg brushed my knee, and he whispered, "I think we'd go well together. I like to bite, too. I'd like to see what else you can do with your teeth."

I had a sexier comeback remark, but I swallowed it down. The professor declared testing time, and we began.

Grayson finished first, but he kept the page open to the last page. When I closed my test, he closed his. After we both handed the test to one of the TAs, we went out together.

Grayson nudged me. "Not bad, right? Almost everything we reviewed was on the test, right?"

"Except for the last five questions." I frowned.

"You've got this." He sounded so encouraging, I almost hugged him. "Piece of cake, only if you read the last chapter of the textbook as I suggested." His eyes narrowed playfully scolding. "Did you read the last chapter, Cams?"

"Cams? Is that my nickname, Gray?" I was glad to divert the attention because, too caught up with Lucas, I hadn't read the textbook.

Grayson's hard chest rose and fell with a chuckle, and then he frowned. "I'm not sure if I like Gray. Makes me sound so old. But whatever turns you on is fine with me."

It was then I realized I knew nothing about him.

"I'm starving," he continued. "Have you tried the Harper Grill by Harper building?"

"No." My tone rose excitedly. "I've been wanting to go."

Grayson's face lit up. "Good. Then let me be the first one to take you. Follow me."

As we strode along the walkway, the trees gave us shade, and the patches of vibrant spring flowers decorated the campus. The soft wind brushed against my ear until we passed groups of students heading to class on their bikes or sprinting to get to class on time.

"I have to say something." I wrung a strand over my ear, peering to the left of me. Grayson matched my slow speed.

"You can tell me anything, Cams." He didn't sound alarmed, but calm.

"I recently broke up with my boyfriend. To make a long story short, I'm not sure what's going to happen." I braced myself, thinking he would leave me there or rant what a terrible person I was for not letting him know from the start, but...

Grayson placed a hand on my shoulder and we halted. "I have a confession to make." He released a breath and stood with his legs apart, holding the strap of his backpack. "I've admired you from afar in Econ class, and I never approached you because I knew you had a boyfriend. I also found out you're not with him anymore."

My face heated. "How?" I glared, angry, not directed at him but at the situation.

"I have friends in Lambda, and I told them I was into you a while back. They told me what happened. Please don't get mad at me." He raised his hands to surrender. "I swear I'm not trying to make a move you're not ready for. I decided to eat at Commons, and when I saw you, I'd thought to ask you to join our study group. I didn't think you would say yes, but I have to admit, I was very happy about it. We are friends, Cams." He pointed to him and me. "I'm asking you to eat as friends, nothing more, unless you want more. I would never try to step in between a broken relationship. I'm not that kind of guy. In fact, I think you'll find me charming and genuine." He smirked. "Most girls fall for my dimples." He pointed at them with a dorky grin. "But like I said, I want to get to know you as friends first. If you don't want to be my friend, I'll understand."

What could I say after that declaration? He told me the truth. He laid it all out. I had to admit, knowing he found me attractive had butterflies swarming in my belly.

"Thank you for telling me the truth. Friends." I nodded to agree. "I can have lunch with a friend."

His stiffened shoulders relaxed as we moved onward. "We're almost there. Do you want to talk about it?"

"Talk about what?" I stepped on a pebble and even wearing my flats, I stumbled.

Grayson caught my fall, his body pressed to mine as his blue eyes locked on my amber ones. Time stood still until something plopped on top of my head, breaking us apart. Something hard, cold, and wet pelted on my head. *Oh my God!*

"What the hell was that?" I reached for my hair, but Grayson gripped my hand.

"No. Don't touch it. It's um—oh damn. Bird—"

"Shit," I finished for him, my cheeks burning. "Shit. Shit. Shit." Peering up to the sky, I searched for the bird. Of course it was too late.

Then we burst into laughter.

"Quick, make a wish," Grayson said unexpectedly.

"What?"

"Hurry."

"Okay, okay. I wish for..." I made a wish in my mind and smiled.

"You know, I've been told if you get shit on and you make a wish, your wish will come true, or was it your luck is about to turn for better." He lit a devilish grin.

"What? I've never heard of that." I leaned closer. "Let me get some on you. You look like you could use some luck."

Grayson backed away chuckling, his hands up to stop me. "Cams, there's nothing to be embarrassed about. You're with a friend."

Then something in me softened, and I appreciated his ability to make me comfortable. "Thanks. I don't feel so bad I think." My lips quirked, trying not to laugh again.

"You can wash it off if you want at the restroom first before we order lunch."

"Sounds like a plan."

I rinsed off a section of my hair and used a paper towel to dry. When I walked out of the restroom, Grayson held a huge smile with his hands inside his pockets, appearing irresistible with those adorable dimples flashing. The sun kissed the tips of his hair, making them lighter brown with streaks of gold.

His perfect face, his sculptured body, he was a Greek god come to life. My heart skipped a beat, and for once, I forgot about Lucas.

We're friends. It's okay to go out to lunch with a good-looking friend, I reminded myself.

CHAPTER ELEVEN
LUNCH DATE
GRAYSON

When Cammy walked out of the restroom, her amber eyes beamed when they set on me. Her hair was a little damp, but still beautiful even slightly disheveled. Damn, her smile gave me warmth everywhere, including a place I didn't want. Or at least not yet, because I knew we could only be friends for now.

"Well, at least you won't smell like bird turd," I casually commented.

Cammy scowled playfully, not at me, but at the situation. "Well, like you said, it's a sign of good luck, so I'll be waiting."

"Just wait and see?" I arched my eyebrows. *Please let the universe be on my side and let me be right.*

I ordered two turkey avocado sandwiches on rye bread. Turned out, Cammy and I liked the same type of sandwiches and chips—salt and vinegar. She offered to pay, but I stood slightly in front of her and paid the bill. After we settled ourselves at a corner table, we ate in comfortable quiet. Cammy seemed to want to be invisible.

That prick, Cams's ex-boyfriend—she deserved someone better. I didn't know him that well, but as an outsider observing, he had blown his chance. Cams didn't know I saw her walk in just as Lucas leaned into that chick.

Cams sipped her soda and met my eyes. "So, where are you from?"

"I'm from New York. Born and raised here. How about you?"

"Same. What high school?"

"John Marshall High." I took a bite of my sandwich.

"No shit? Your school was our rival." Her eyes twinkled, appearing more gold than amber in the sunlight.

"Well, what do you know?" I opened the bag of chips for us and offered her to take the first piece. She reached in. "What a small world."

"Yup. It sure is. Any siblings?" The chip crunched inside her mouth, and then she reached to take more. "These are delicious."

I tilted the bag toward her. "I have an older brother. He's happily married with a son. Want to see a picture of my nephew?" Without waiting for a reply, I took the photo out of my wallet and passed it to her.

"Oh, he's so cute. Look at those dimples." Cammy met my gaze. "Your brother has them, too, I'm guessing?"

"Grant does, like me." I shrugged, feeling shy for the first time. Cammy's eyes on me had me a bit nervous. "He lives in New York, too. He's a lawyer at a big firm downtown, and my sister-in-law is a pediatrician." *Too much information, Grayson.*

"A lawyer and a doctor? Wow. And your parents?"

"My dad is a business lawyer as well. He's an in-house counsel for a big investment firm. He was so happy when my brother told him he wanted to be a lawyer just like him. My mom was an elementary school teacher. She retired soon after I was born. How about you?" I took a long gulp of my soda.

"I got accepted to NYU's teacher certification program."

"You did? That's awesome. Congratulations. So, you'll be here as well." I raised my arms for emphasis. "The universe is telling us we were meant to be friends."

She smiled and continued. "My parents are divorced. My mom is a nurse and my stepdad is a doctor. I have a younger sister who's graduating from high school this year."

I slightly dipped my head. "Congrats are in order for the Connor family. Two daughters graduating."

Cammy took the last bite of her sandwich and crinkled the wrapper. "Thank you for my lunch. It was very sweet of you."

"That's what friends are for." Idiotic. I could've kicked myself. Couldn't I think of something better to say?

"Friends." She paused on the word. "I like that." She glanced at her watch. "I hate to leave my friend alone, but I have to get to work. Gus, my manager, gets all pissy when I'm even a second late."

I took her trash and mine. "I'll walk you there."

She reached for the wrapper, but then she placed her hand down her side. "You don't have to take my trash. I can do it. And you don't have to walk me to work. I'm sure you have better things to do."

"Nothing is better than spending time with you."

Cammy's cheeks gleamed slightly pink. "It's clear across campus."

"I know. But I'm just a guy hoping maybe one day we can be more than friends." I should have punched myself, or I should have let her punch me. I was an ass. She was hurting and I sprung my words on her as if she didn't have anything else to worry about.

I didn't mean to remind her of that, but it was so easy to talk to her. Turning my back toward her to toss the trash away, I didn't give her a chance to reply.

CHAPTER TWELVE
AT WORK
CAMMY

Grayson was so sweet, such a gentleman, but his words surprised me. *I'm just a guy hoping maybe one day we can be more than friends.*

How could I not swoon over those words? But I wasn't ready to move on or let Lucas completely go. Confused, I did what I did best when I didn't want to make a decision: I pretended everything was fine.

"Grayson." Gus's smile was too big for his face. "Cammy. You're here on time." He waved and attention went to Grayson. "You should walk Cammy to work every day. Are you hungry, Grayson? I can whip you up something. I'll even pile it on for you."

I rolled my eyes at Gus, plopped my backpack under the counter, and checked the cash register to make sure it was all good to go. Actually, my nerves were fried. A part of me worried Lucas would find out I had eaten with another guy and might get mad. It was none of his business, I reminded myself.

"Actually, I'm going to skip. Cams and I had lunch, but thank you."

Gus's eyebrow hiked higher than I'd ever seen before. "Oh, really." His eyes flashed to mine with a look that said *tell me more.*

"Anyway." Grayson shoved his hands inside his jeans pockets, and his lips perked as if he was either thinking of something to say or was wondering about something. "I had a wonderful time, friend. Maybe we can do it again soon." The way his hands braced against the counter, his toned biceps were hard to miss when he leaned forward. Even Gus drooled from the other end. "Have a good day, Cams. See you in class. I'll save you a seat."

"You too. See you in class." I tried to sound neutral and not flirty.

"Those were the sexiest words I've heard in a long time." Gus stood next to me, staring at Grayson walk away. "And he's got the sexiest ass I've ever seen."

I'm not looking. I'm not looking. Shit, I was already gawking.

I frowned. "Don't you have work to do? Go back to your side."

I had expected a sly comment, but instead, he was grinning and waving at someone. Grayson had turned back, his eyes set on mine, just before he exited.

The second he was no longer in the building, Gus shifted his attention to me. "What happened? How did you get a date with him?"

I glanced around the quiet food court. "It wasn't a date. We're friends. We have a class together, and after the test, we went out to eat."

I dusted a smudge from the cash register, keeping myself busy. I didn't want Gus to see any expression on my face.

Gus lightly tapped my shoulder. "Was anyone else there?"

"It's none of your business, but no." I checked the containers filled with tomatoes, lettuce, onion, rice, beans, chicken, beef, shredded pork, and sauces.

Gus crossed his arms. "You keep telling yourself that. Oh, by the way, Lucas stopped by just before you came in with Mr. Hot Man."

My eyes shot to him, my heart thundering. "What did he say?"

Gus took out the tortillas and placed them neatly on the counter. "Nothing much." He scowled. "He was grouchy and rude. He wanted to know when you were coming to work. Because of his attitude, I told him you weren't working today."

I didn't know whether to be annoyed with Gus or hug him. "Thanks," I said curtly.

Gus pushed back his hair. "I don't like bullies with attitudes, and I especially don't like cheaters."

I froze when I reached the register, seeing a customer heading toward us. "How do you know what he did?"

I wanted to hide from embarrassment. Though I didn't do anything wrong, I suddenly realized one of the reasons why I couldn't go back with Lucas wasn't just because he cheated on me, but also because of my pride.

The whole damn campus knew what Lucas had done. Of course people would talk, especially among the fraternities and sororities.

Gus placed a soft hand over mine, and he gave me a compassionate expression. "I think you know the answer."

CHAPTER THIRTEEN
SICK
CAMMY

After working my eight-hour shift, I was beyond exhausted. The twinkling, beautiful stars were apparent in the clear night sky, surrounding the full moon. As I took in the serene beauty, I shivered and entered my apartment.

"Hey, Cammy. How was your day?" Leah peered up from her laptop and smiled.

I slouched next to her on the sofa with my legs apart. "I've never been this tired and cold. I think I'm coming down with something."

Leah shifted in her seat and angled her body toward me. "Oh no. Maybe you're getting what I got. If you caught it from me I'm so sorry."

Leaning my head back, I placed my hand over my forehead. "It's not your fault, Leah. It's probably from lack of sleep. A part of me wants to dump Lucas's ass, but we've been together for a year. I don't know if I can let him go."

"Obviously." Leah reached for me, causing me to sit straighter and meet her gaze. "I know how you feel. And you shouldn't have to make that kind of decision right now. It's been like what, less than a week? Lucas better not be giving you a hard time. It was his fault. If he truly cares for you, he'll wait. But if a part of you doubts this relationship, you might want to consider leaving him."

"I know," I sighed, grabbing a throw pillow to hug it. "I wish things were simple."

Leah punched her fingers along the computer keyboard and then faced me. "Speaking of Lucas. The dude came by."

"What did he want?" The room suddenly felt cooler.

"The usual. He wanted to know where you were and what time you would come home."

I rubbed at my temple, a headache forming. "What did you say?"

Her lips twitched, radiating a satisfied smile. "I said you were out on a hot date and he should screw himself."

Blood drained out of me. "Leah."

"I'm just kidding." She smirked. "I said you would be home later this evening, and I slammed the door on his face. I told him he should have kept his ugly lips to himself and he better have kept his dick inside his pants or I would cut it off."

My lips parted in shock, but what was I shocked about? Leah spoke her mind, and she didn't care what others thought of her. Sometimes I wished I could be like her. Stronger. Bolder.

"Do you still have the Nyquil I gave you?" I rested my head on the armrest, trembling. "I don't feel so good, Leah."

"Crap." Leah placed her hand over my forehead. "You're burning up. I'll be right back." Leah only took a few steps when the door chimed. "Who the hell is that?" she cursed under her breath. "Great timing."

I couldn't tell who it was from her voice.

"Lucas. Come in." Leah peeked over her shoulder and locked her wicked, up to no good, eyes to mine.

What was Leah up to? She sounded too pleased for his company. Ugh. Didn't she know I didn't want to see him?

"Lucas, it's not a good time." My fever gripped me into shivers.

Lucas ignored my words as usual and sat across from me. His eyes flamed with anger and his fists tightened. "Cammy. What the hell?"

I blinked. *What's wrong with him?* I stared and stared, unable to part my lips to speak.

"What?" I finally spat. "I don't feel well. I have a fever. Can we please talk when I'm better?"

"Are you sleeping with him?" He speared his eyes to mine.

"What? Who are you talking about?" Heat flushed through my neck and my face, mixed with rage and fever.

"Grayson. You told me you wanted space, but you're parading around the campus with him like he's your boyfriend."

I inhaled a breath and seethed, "He's my friend. I have friends, you know. You're allowed to have friends but I'm not?"

"That's not the point, Cammy." He raked his hair back, clenching his jaw. "What do you want me to do? You want me to get down on my knees and beg? I'll do whatever you want. Just give us another chance."

The ache in my head and stomach took a turn for the worse. "I don't feel good, Lucas." My head spun and the walls closed in tighter.

Leah handed me Nyquil to drink. "Here, sweetie. Maybe this will help." She whirled to Lucas. "She's not feeling well. Either take care of her or get out. But don't make it worse."

As if something finally clicked, understanding registered on his face. "Do you need anything?" Lucas asked, his tone and expression finally softening.

"No." I spread across the sofa and closed my eyes. I was tired, angry, and I didn't want to talk to him.

How dare he accuse me of having a boyfriend behind his back? And to think I was worried about his feelings and reputation with his frat brothers. I wanted to toss my glass of water at him. But I was too tired and too sick.

There was no fight in me. I didn't care if he stayed or left. The ringing in my head and my temperature changing from hot and cold took everything out of me.

"Let me help you to your bed." Leah's voice. Her hand on my forehead felt like ice.

Then another pair of hands supported me. Someone took off my flats and covered me.

CHAPTER FOURTEEN
HOMEMADE SOUP
CAMMY

I drifted in and out of sleep for two days. Leah helped me drink water and sip some soup. Through the hazy slumber, a male's voice sounded from a distance.

A part of me hoped it was Lucas so I could prove to Leah that he truly cared for me. If he had stayed or at least came every day to check up on me, I would give him another chance.

By the third day, my fever finally relented, and my stiff muscles eased. Apparently, my flu was worse than Leah's.

Laughter and murmurs came from the other side of the door. *Lucas?* Leah was laughing with him? Impossible.

Leah didn't like Lucas, and if it were up to her, I wouldn't be with him. But you don't get to choose who you love. Love chooses for you.

I sat up when a soft knock on the door reverberated, and before I could say a word, the door swung open.

"Cammy, you're awake." Leah smiled, coming toward me with a bed tray.

"You are too good to me," I said. "What would I do without you?"

"You did the same for me, roomie. Just paying you back. Besides, what are friends for if you can't use them?" She snickered.

After she placed the tray in a standing position across my lap, she sat on the edge of the bed with a beaming smile.

"You seem happy today," I commented. "What's going on? Did you meet someone? I heard a guy's voice." My stomach rumbled from the aroma and the sight of what appeared to be a homemade chicken noodle soup when I took off the plate that kept the bowl warm. Steam rose like ghost mists. "Did you cook this?"

Leah fanned a hand to her chest. "Me? Cook that? Hell no. You know I burn everything. Besides, I would never touch raw whole chicken."

True. I'd never seen Leah cook. "Then where did you get this soup?"

"From the chef," a manly voice answered.

I slowly craned my head toward the threshold. Grayson had his hands inside his jean pockets, leaning his back against the door. His blue T-shirt accentuated his eyes even more.

"Grayson?" I swallowed. "How? When? What are you doing here?" I tried not to sound too surprised.

"When you didn't come to class, I got worried. I figured you would at least come to class to find out what you got on your test. You don't seem to be the type to ditch." He chuckled lightly.

Leah slid off the bed. "I told Grayson you're sick. Well, you're better now, but you were sick. Last night he came back with homemade chicken soup. I fed you some, but you probably don't remember because you were so drugged with Nyquil. You slept forever."

I glanced between Leah and Grayson. "Thank you both for taking care of me. I really didn't want to call my mom. And Grayson, you didn't have to go out of your way to make me soup."

My stomach already felt full, not from soup, but from his kindness, for caring. I felt a sharp pain in my heart. Lucas might have helped tuck me in bed, most likely from Leah's harsh demand, but he didn't stay. And he had never cooked for me.

You deserve someone that cares about you when you're sick. You deserve someone that walks you home. Leah's words echoed in my mind. I did deserve someone better than Lucas, but regardless, Lucas had a year ahead of Grayson.

Lucas and I shared a year of good and bad. I couldn't just toss him away, couldn't let go yet. But a part of my heart tugged toward Grayson. *Help me.*

"Well." Leah's voice broke Grayson's and my stare. "I better get going. I have a class in a half hour." Leah winked at me. "Have fun." Then she turned to Grayson. "Can you put the tray back into the kitchen for me when Cammy is done? And thanks for the soup again. That was very sweet of you."

Grayson rubbed the back of his head and grinned. "You're welcome."

"Cammy is sick. No kissing." Leah stepped out of my view, leaving the two of us alone.

My face burned and I almost choked on the spoonful of soup I had just sipped. Grayson's face blanched and his eyes widened.

"You don't have to wait until I finish my soup, Grayson. I'm sure you have other important things to do. And again, thank you so much for the delicious soup," I rambled, nervous at how much I enjoyed his company.

He shrugged. "It's my pleasure to watch you eat and keep you company. And you're welcome. I had to show you my awesome skills. Besides being really good at playing Frogger, I'm also a good cook. My mother forced me to learn before I left for college. She said it was a sure way to win a girl's heart." He considered his words with a blink. "I mean we're friends. I didn't make soup because of what she said. You were very sick, and I'm glad to help."

"Thank you," I said sincerely and then took another spoonful. "So you just going to stand there and watch me eat or are you going to join me?"

"Leah and I already ate together." He gestured out the door with the tilt of his head. "In the dining area. As friends."

I snorted inwardly. "Then would you like to keep me company? You could sit on my desk chair instead of standing. You're making me nervous."

"Oh, sorry." He took a few steps and glanced at my bookshelf. "When do you have time to read?"

I wiped my mouth with a paper napkin. "I read those during summer." I scratched an itch on my nose. "I know you used to be in a fraternity. Why did you de-pledge?"

His eyes widened in surprise, probably not expecting that question out of the blue. Taking my desk chair, he sat, his chest facing the back of the chair, and scrubbed his face. Finding that quite sexy, I craned my neck sideways.

"I de-pledged when I realized it was taking too much time away from my ex-girlfriend. We fought a lot because pledging took too much time away from our relationship. She wasn't happy about the social events and me meeting other sorority girls. I understood. If the situation was the opposite, I would have felt the same. It would be a different story if she was already in a sorority, but she wasn't. People who are not in the system don't really understand. But after I de-pledged for her, she dumped me."

"What? Seriously?" I took more sips of the soup and listened attentively.

"Yup." He tapped his feet on the carpet. "It was better for me anyway. It was fun the first year and I met a lot of people, but I probably would have eventually de-pledged or become less active. To tell you the truth, it's been a while since I've dated. I've just been pouring myself into my studies and planning for my future."

"Smart choice. There are no do-overs. Now is the time." I frowned. "I sound like I'm preaching, don't I?"

Grayson snorted. "I think it's cute."

I blushed and drank more of my soup. Then I cleared my throat when I felt his eyes solely on me, feeling naked under his.

"So how did you do on the test?"

He scratched the side of his neck and shifted in his seat. "Do you want the truth or a lie?"

"Grayson," I chided. "Don't lie. It's okay if you didn't do as well as me." I smiled mischievously.

He chuckled. "You don't even know what you got on the test."

"True. So what did you get?"

"I missed one." His lips slanted into a pout and those dimples became more apparent.

Holy shit! Put that lip back up.

"Truth or a lie?" I said.

"What do you think?" He furrowed his brow.

"What do I get if I'm right?" Dangerous question.

He considered my question, squinting his eyes. "I have to cook dinner for you. And if I win, I have to cook dinner for you."

I arched my eyebrows in confusion. "Did I hear you—"

Before I could say another word, he said, "Yes you did. Either way, I get to cook for you. From what Leah told me, it doesn't sound like either of you can cook."

"What?" I squealed. "Leah can't cook, but I can. Somewhat. Sort of." I pouted, giving him my innocent face.

From the way his eyes darkened, I swear I thought he was going to dash over and kiss me.

"So what's the verdict?" I said quickly before we got too carried away. We were friends, I reminded myself and did a mental check to see if I had flirted or had led him on.

"So, what's your answer, Cams?" He emphasized my name.

"You told me a lie," I answered, but it sounded more like a question.

"I won."

"Liar." I giggled. "Where's your proof? I want proof."

He came to me in five steps, stopping next to the bed. I became breathless at the size of his broad shoulders, his hard muscles, and just his overall presence.

Noting I had finished the soup, he took the tray off my bed and set it on the floor. With his hands planted on either side of me by my waist, he leaned closer.

Oh dear God. I held my breath when he bit his bottom lip and his eyes lowered to mine. I knew that look in his eyes. It was the same expression I was pretty sure I was giving him.

"What did you call me?" His tone was soft, and though he tried to be playful, I was sure his mind went elsewhere with me in his thoughts.

An incoherent word left my mouth, something close to a word liar when I tried to reply. Grayson blinked and his eyes shifted to the TV screen, as if he realized our stare seemed far too intimate, crossing the line of friendship. He reached inside his back pocket and took out a piece of paper and opened it for me to see.

"You didn't win." I jabbed his chest.

"Ouch." He jerked back, acting all cute and hurt.

"You lied." I narrowed my eyes at him. "You didn't miss one. You got them all right. So I won. By the way, congrats."

After he folded his test, he shoved it back and shrugged. "No big deal."

With his face close to mine, I pounded a pillow at his face. Staggering sideways, his eyes shot wide.

"No big deal? The professor even said no one would get a hundred percent. You did great. You should be proud."

Grayson began to wiggle his fingers, his eyes promising... oh no. "You threw a pillow at my face. Now it's my..." Those were the only words I heard. Grayson's fingers poked my sides.

"Stop," I breathed, laughing so hard I kicked the blanket aside.

He stopped and I stopped. His hands locked my arms over my shoulders. His eyes roamed my face, and then at last my eyes. Something sweet and kind and hurt flickered in them. So close. His lips were so close to mine. My breathing quickened and lust filled my senses.

"You're lucky you're sick. I stopped because I don't want to tire you."

"I'd like to know the other ways you make a girl tired." The words left before I could stop them, but it felt so right and natural with Grayson. But I shouldn't have said it.

His eyes beamed in wicked delight. "Oh, believe me. They're too exhausted to remember their own name after I'm done."

I didn't know if I was breathing. "Oh, really?" I swallowed.

Slowly, so very slowly, he moved closer and closer as I savored the scent of his cologne. His lips veered up and softly planted a kiss on my forehead, letting go of my pinned arms. Then he took the blanket and covered me.

"I get to cook you dinner as a friend. That's a win for me. Get some sleep, Cams."

After he grabbed my tray, he headed for the door. Just before he was out of my sight, he stopped by the threshold and glanced over his shoulder.

"Don't check out my ass, Cams, just because I checked out yours."

Shit! How did he know?

Scooting lower and raising the blanket closer to my neck, my face burned. I was in so much trouble.

CHAPTER FIFTEEN
BACK TO WORK
CAMMY

"Welcome back, stranger." Gus seemed to be in a good mood from the sound of his tone. "How are you feeling?"

Leah had called Gus to let him know I had the flu.

"I'm feeling better. Thanks for asking."

Rushing to my spot, I surveyed the lunch crowd. After a long morning listening to a lecture, I felt overwhelmed. Then I remembered I hadn't eaten anything that morning because I got up late. I badly needed a coffee or to eat something. If only I could just go across the court to the bakery and get a drink.

I cringed at the sight of Lucas's frat brothers and shrunk a little lower when Lucas saw me. Shifting my attention, I rung up the customer and then another, aware of his presence and his eyes on me as he strode my way and... *Crap!* So was Grayson from the other side, but he was closer, all smiles and dimples and not aware of Lucas. I stiffened.

"Hey, Cams." Grayson grinned. "What are you—"

"Do you mind, Grayson," Lucas sneered beside him, cutting him off. "I would like to talk to my girl, whom you've been trying to steal."

He didn't ask how I was feeling? Not a single word about my well-being.

"He isn't doing anything," I spat.

Grayson took a step back like a perfect gentleman, shaking his head.

"Do you mind, Lucas?" Gus appeared beside me. "If you want to talk to Cammy, get in line and buy something. You're holding the line." Gus only scolded Lucas and grinned at Grayson.

I took care of the customer who glanced at all four of us, looking uncomfortable, and then turned to Lucas. "I'm at work. Let's talk later."

His nostrils flared, and his tone dipped lower. "You were willing to talk to that guy behind me, but you won't talk to me? Okay, I see."

"Stop it, Lucas. You're wrong." I shook my head. "He's not making a scene, but you are."

He threw up his hands. "I can't deal with this shit anymore, Cammy. Either we make it work or we're done."

My jaw dropped. *How dare he?* My eyes burned and heat flared in my body. "I'm not talking to you right now. Go away and cool down." I was already exhausted, but seeing Lucas drained me.

Lucas's eyes diverted to Grayson with daggers. His expression told me I was not in the wrong. Lucas shouldn't have shown up and demanded like that, especially at work. Unprofessional. Again, he thought of only himself and what he wanted.

Lucas stormed away, and Grayson retreated, taking small, backward steps, examining me as if silently asking if I was okay.

After I finished with the customer who had to witness the bickering, Grayson came over.

"I'm so sorry. I didn't mean to get him upset. I didn't know he was here," Grayson went on.

"Stop, Grayson." I almost reached out to him. "It's not your fault and please don't apologize. Lucas thinks he has the right to demand my attention whenever he wants. Did you have a question?"

He rubbed at his temple. "Oh. Here." He placed a paper mug on the counter. "It's for you." His eyes set on my face as if he could read through me. "You looked exhausted when I came in, so I thought you might need some coffee."

Tears pooled in my eyes, and I lowered my gaze. I had let Lucas's words slice through my heart, and here was Grayson, being so sweet and giving me what I wished for, like my angel mending it back up.

"I really need this, Grayson. You've saved my day. You're my hero. Thank you so much." I offered a warm smile and I savored the first hot sip.

Grayson's dimples answered my gratitude. "There's one condition."

I took another sip, moaning softly with my eyes closed, breathing in a deep breath. "What's the condition?" I asked, opening my eyes.

Grayson ran his hand ever so slowly down his face. "Actually, there are two now. First, you have to watch *Mission Impossible* with me tonight, or tomorrow, or this weekend, as friends of course. You choose. And second" — he leaned closer to whisper in my ear — "don't make that sound. You give me naughty thoughts, Cams. Friend or no friend, you have that kind of power over me."

I flushed with warmth and pressed my lips together from laughing. "Okay. Since you saved my day, I'll watch *Mission Impossible* with you. I've been wanting to watch it for some time. But I have to warn you. I get a bit jumpy at the suspenseful parts."

Grayson twitched his lips and his eyes twinkled with amusement. "Such a baby. But don't worry. I'll make sure you're safe. Besides cooking, I have a special talent. I'm good at giving comfort."

"Are you now?" I snorted. "Good to know. Next time an alien comes to hunt me, I'll make sure to let you know."

His eyes lit up brighter. "You saw *Independence Day?*"

"Heck yeah. My family and I went on the day it came out."

"I think I love you even more. I mean as friends," he corrected.

A pause. The room seemed quieter. "Anyway, I should go. You're working, and I've taken enough of your time. Gus keeps looking at me. He's smiling, but I think he's trying to tell me to get going."

I smiled. Little did Grayson know Gus had a crush on him. "Thanks again for my coffee." I raised the paper mug to him.

"My pleasure to take care of you, Cams." He winked and left.

"Not only does he smell divine, girl, he's got it bad for you." Gus lightly bumped his hip to mine. A drop of coffee spilled on my hand. "Sorry."

I sucked it up. "No worries. And he does not. We're friends."

Gus furrowed his brow. "There is no such thing as *friends*. A guy doesn't just bring a friend coffee or ask her to go see a movie as *friends*."

I shrugged, dismissing Gus's words. He had no idea what went on between Grayson and me.

I nudged his shoulder. "What do you know? You just want to take him to bed."

He gave a wicked smile. "You bet I do."

I snorted and got back to work when a customer came by.

Caroline. Shit!

I played it cool and held my chin high, but my heart pounded hard against my rib cage. She met my eyes once and diverted her attention to something else.

"Eleven," I said flatly.

A ten and a five landed on the counter. I took it and placed four bills on the same spot. I had no intention of our hands brushing. She cleared her throat. When I didn't pay attention to her, she cleared her throat again. I peered under my eyelashes and finally met her eyes.

"I'm sorry." Her index finger nervously tapped on the tray. "I was a bit tipsy. It didn't mean anything."

Why does everyone want to talk to me at work?

Thankfully, Gus went to the back room so I had a little time to talk. I didn't know what to say. It felt so awkward to be confronted, and I didn't like conflicts, but I was beyond enraged. Hurt and anger boiled inside me, stronger than before. And I had a fervent urge to say my piece.

"I don't know what you want me to say. Did Lucas put you up to this?"

She stiffened. "No. I just want to make it clear that I'm not a slut and I'm not a boyfriend stealer."

I crossed my arms, and with a sassy tone, I sputtered, "Don't give yourself too much credit, you haven't stolen him. He told me you meant nothing to him. He's begging for me to take him back. I think I'll make him grovel a bit more."

Her eyes shot wide and she kept quiet for only a heartbeat. "I'm not talking to you because I'm trying to break you two up, but you don't know Lucas well. I think you trust him way too much. You don't know what he's like at the social gatherings."

I growled under my breath. *How dare she tell me things I didn't need to hear to confuse me.* "I think I know my own boyfriend, whom I've known longer than you."

Caroline took the change and picked up her tray. "All I'm saying is that you seem like a really nice person. He doesn't deserve you. You really need to start asking questions about his loyalty toward you." With that, she walked away.

My blood pressure spiked. I couldn't breathe. Lucas went to plenty of Greek social events. I knew he drank, but I trusted him. I had to. I never questioned his faithfulness. But if he had cheated on me during the events, his brothers would never tell.

I began to wonder about the year we'd been together. *If what Caroline said were true … Had I been that blind?*

Maybe I had closed my eyes, not wanting to see the truth. Leah thought Lucas wasn't good enough for me. Did she suspect, or had she actually seen things?

I shivered, noting the time. Feeling sick to my stomach at the revelation unfolding, I wanted to vomit right then and there. Five minutes until someone else would take over my shift.

The floor began to spin. *No air. No air. No air.* Gripping the counter, I inhaled deep breaths. Then a gentle hand rested on my shoulder. Gus's hand.

"Cammy. Go home. You've had a long day."

I agreed and went home.

"What's wrong, Cammy?" Leah asked when I entered. She took a step into her bedroom, but she came out and sat on the sofa instead.

I slammed the door behind me, plopped next to her, and told her everything.

"Do you believe her?" she asked.

"I don't know," I answered softly.

"The only way you'll know for sure is by talking to Lucas. Except I doubt he would tell you the truth."

I leaned back into the sofa and stretched my legs on top of the coffee table. "Are we still on for girls' night out tomorrow?"

Leah's eyes lit up. "We sure are. It's been so long. I can't wait."

"Me too."

Leaning my head onto her shoulder, I thought about calling Lucas but decided to wait until after tomorrow. Maybe I knew it would be our last conversation and I was stalling.

CHAPTER SIXTEEN
PARTY WITH FRIENDS
CAMMY

"Here's to us." Tiffany raised her beer bottle, her green eyes beaming. "We're on the last stretch to graduation.

"Four years flew by so fast. I'm going to miss our girls' nights out." Julie frowned, her upraised arm holding a bottle next to Tiffany's.

"Here's to the future," Vanessa said.

"I'm so happy and thankful for our friendship that got us through breakups, heartaches, and everything that was terrible," Valerie added.

"We've all been through ups and downs the past four years, but our friendship stayed strong," Leah said last.

I finished our toast by saying, "Congrats to Tiffany for getting into one of the best optometry graduate schools. I'm coming to see you when I need glasses." I snorted. "Congrats to Julie for getting into Harvard Law School. I hope I don't have to ask you for your services.

Congrats to Vanessa on her new job as a human resources assistant. And to my bestie, my roommate, I'm so happy we'll be continuing to live together and see where life takes us."

Tiffany narrowed her eyes at me. "And congrats Cammy for getting into the teaching program. I don't know why you would want to work with kids."

We shared a good laugh and clinked our glasses. The six of us met our freshman year during orientation. Living in the same dorm had helped nurture our friendship, and we'd been best friends since then.

Julie leaned into me and spoke over the music. "Have you dumped his sorry ass yet?"

"No talking secrets. I want to hear all the gossip." Tiffany waved a hand, her face slightly flushing from the alcohol.

After dinner, we decided to hang out at Jo Jo's Bar and Grill across from campus. One of the bartenders had seemed to take an interest in Leah, and I believe she did him, though she wouldn't admit it. Sometimes, he would give us a round of free drinks. But he wasn't working today.

"I wanted to know if Cammy dumped Lucas," Julie said.

"Dump him and get a new one that can keep his mouth to himself." Tiffany shrugged. "You deserve someone who treats you like he can't live without you."

"We all do." Valerie tapped her bottle.

My mind went silent and heartache began to build. "But how do you let go?"

Julie murmured, "You just do it. You just say goodbye and don't look back and know that there is someone else meant for you out there waiting for you, too." Julie had recently broken up with her boyfriend of two years. She knew my pain.

"That's why you date around, like me." Valerie bumped her shoulder to mine. "After the honeymoon stage is over is when you really get to know the person. Sometimes you match, and sometimes it's time to say see ya later."

"Do you want to see my glamour shot? I had them done a week ago." Tiffany took out a picture of her.

I leaned closer. "You look beautiful."

"Gorgeous." Valerie winked. "I should do one."

Tiffany shrugged. "You should. We all should."

Leah lightly tapped her shoe to mine under the table and gestured to the entrance. Blood drained out of me as my friends and I observed. Lucas and his buddies strode in like they owned the place, right to a table of girls opposite our spot.

Lucas hadn't seen me yet. We were in the corner under the dim light. I tried to hide, letting my hair cascade down my face, but I peeked through the layers.

Lucas hugged some of the girls and he sat next to a brunette. Her hand slid down his arm, and the way he ogled her told me more than words could say. They were smiling at each other as if... *Oh God.* I felt nauseous.

Was this the way Lucas acted when he went to his social functions without me? Did everyone see the way he was with other girls except for me? The picture seemed clear now. And after what I had seen, there was no chance in hell I would give him a second chance.

My friends whirled away from Lucas, disgust boiling in their eyes, and spun to me with sympathetic expressions.

"Let's get out of here." Leah raised her hand to get the waitress's attention to get our bill.

My friends agreed. I didn't know what to say, but I didn't want to be in the same vicinity with—I couldn't say his name. I gave Leah a twenty from my wallet and didn't glance back.

If he truly was sorry and wanted us to have a second chance, he wouldn't be friendly with any girl. Perhaps seeing me with Grayson, he thought he had no chance of getting me back. Or maybe his mask had finally been revealed after a year. It didn't matter. After what I had just seen, I would never be able to trust him.

"We should walk around them." Leah stood up after counting the money. "I want to see the look on Lucas's face when he sees us."

Tiffany stroked my arm. "Is this what you want to do, Cammy?"

All eyes flashed to me.

At first, I didn't know. I wanted to hide when I saw him, and then I wanted to punch him a second later when he flirted with that girl. The insecure part of me wanted to run away. But a new me, one who'd had enough, one who finally opened her eyes rose out of her seat.

"I have a score to settle." I marched to Lucas, my friends behind me.

Lucas spotted me. His eyes widened with shock. His hands lifted from the girl and he stood up, stiffening, and parted his mouth to speak.

Grabbing a full glass of water, I dumped it in his face. "We're done. I don't ever want to see you again." With that, I strode out the door with my head up, never looking back.

Behind me, I could have sworn I heard snorts and curses from his friends.

CHAPTER SEVENTEEN
FIRST KISS
CAMMY

A Week Later

"No, no, no. Don't go in there," I murmured into the palms of my hands, almost choking on popcorn I had chewed. Thankfully, we sat in the farthest back row and only one other couple sat toward the front. The campus theater was never crowded, especially the last show and in the middle of the week.

"This is the best part. Don't close your eyes," Grayson whispered into my ear.

"Easy for you to say. You already know what happens." I lightly smacked his arm, and then partially covered my eyes.

My heart thudded as the bad guy snuck behind the hero. When he spun, they exchanged gunshots. I flinched and almost screamed. Instead, I ducked toward Grayson, my forehead touching the hard curve of his biceps.

"He's gone," Grayson whispered. "Nothing to be afraid of." He stroked my hair.

I felt like an idiot. I was such a scaredy cat.

When I peered up to meet his blue eyes, those eyes that sparkled with tenderness and everything that screamed what a man should be, I realized I didn't want to lose him. He had been there for me as a friend, but most of all he waited patiently for me. To him, I was worth the wait, and that meant everything to me.

There were two kinds of men in the world, mom had told me once. There was the kind that loved women so much that his eyes wandered and the kind that would love only one woman devotedly.

I had thought Lucas was the latter, but apparently he wasn't. And a deep part of me had known he wasn't meant for me, but I couldn't let him go. I was glad I did, for I realized the guy whose arms were around me, giving me comfort, was meant for me.

Grayson had been in the shadows all along, and fate had brought us together at the right time. Though my heart still ached from Lucas's betrayal, from the loss of love and what we had shared, I was ready to move on, but slowly.

I could give Grayson a piece of my heart, small pieces of me at a time, but I couldn't jump in and give it to him wholly. But without a doubt, whatever was happening with Grayson and me, it felt right.

"Grayson." Saying his name seemed a bit more intimate this time.

"Yes." He met my gaze with those bedroom, seductive eyes.

Rising up to get a better angle, I bored my eyes into his with no guilt, and I kissed him. His lips tasted like popcorn and soda.

He stiffened at first, no doubt from shock, but then he pressed me tighter to his chest and gently kissed me back, and it was how I imagined our first kiss would feel—sweet and tender—our lips moving to the steady rhythm until he pulled back.

"Are you sure?" He blinked, unbelieving. "Are you ready?"

I nodded, biting my bottom lip. "Yes. But we need to take things slow. I think I fell for you the moment you asked me to join your study group. If Lucas had not been in my life, I would have wanted to be together from the start."

Grayson's eyes heated and darkened lustfully. "I think I fell in love with you when you stared at my ass when I walked away."

I narrowed my eyes at him. "I didn't stare at your butt."

He cocked an eyebrow, forcing me to think again.

"Okay, but Gus stared at your ass first. You have a nice ass. I'd like to squeeze it soon."

Grayson let out a snort. "I like to squeeze, too. We make a perfect couple. But no more talking. I need to declare you're mine. Forget the movie." With one swift movement, he had me in his lap, and then he kissed me like there was no tomorrow.

After the movie, he walked me to my place. Leah was seated on the sofa watching an episode of *Friends*.

"How was the movie?" she narrowed her eyes at me as if to tell me she knew something was up.

"Good. Better than I had anticipated." My body warmed and my cheeks heated from the memory of our kiss.

Grayson cleared his throat.

I gave him a pointed look.

"I should get going. See ya later, Leah." Grayson walked backward toward the door, never taking his eyes off me. "I'll call you later tonight." He twisted the doorknob, but then he paused. He took three long strides to me, cupped my cheeks, and kissed me with all of him. When he let go he said, "Dream of us. I have been every night since the day I met you."

He left, leaving me breathless and my heart soaring to the sky.

"Holy cow, Cammy. I'm so happy for you. He's the smartest choice you've ever made," Leah burst out excitedly.

I scowled playfully, but just before I was going to tell Leah the details of how our date went, the doorbell chimed. Thinking it was Grayson, I opened the door — and froze. My smile faded and my heart hammered into overdrive.

What the hell does he want?

I wasn't in the mood to fight, and I wasn't going to let him ruin my special night. He wasn't going to take away this joyful sensation I finally found again.

"What do you want?" I hissed.

"I just want to talk. Will you come with me?"

I shot a glance to Leah. Her frown was bigger than mine. I took a step and shut the door behind me. "We can talk here."

Lucas rubbed the nape of his neck and exhaled a heavy sigh. "I'm sorry, Cammy. It's not the way it should have ended between us. You did mean the world to me, and I hate that you hate me."

I crossed my arms and leaned into the building structure to give me support. Not all of his words were present tense, so I let him continue.

"You were an amazing girlfriend. You've always been there for me. You deserve someone who will treat you the way you should be treated. I realized I'm not the guy for you. I'm spoiled. I get what I want. I'm not ready to settle down. I should have said something to you about two months ago, but I couldn't let you go. You are special and one of kind. One day, when I'm ready, I hope to find someone like you. I will always have a special place for you in my heart."

Tears streamed down my face, not because I was hurt or wanted Lucas back, but because he cared enough to let me know how he felt, he knew he was in the wrong, and that our one year together did mean something to him. Many times I wondered if it was something I had done, but he erased my doubt.

I nodded and wiped my tears. There were no words for me to express. I had said some horrible things when we fought, and I humiliated him in front of his friends and acted childishly. In two months, we would graduate and I might never see him again. Now, knowing Lucas was not the one I wanted forever with, letting go seemed easier.

"Thank you, Lucas. You will have a special place in my heart, too."

When Lucas reached for my hand, I let him. Tears glistened in his eyes. "Be happy, Cammy. I wish you only the best." He kissed the top of my forehead. "You will always be my baby. I will always love you."

"I wish you well, too." I meant every word.

My heart was a tangle of emotion. The ending of one relationship and a beginning of a new one. I was glad Lucas had come to see me, and though we had been a mess toward the end, this confession between us helped give me closure.

Lucas's words began to sew me back up, but Grayson's love would heal the wound and ensure there were no scars.

After I watched Lucas disappear into the elevator, I went inside and sat next to Leah.

"What did the douchebag want?" Leah offered me a spoon. She held a tub of ice cream.

I took a spoonful of chocolate and savored the cool taste in my mouth. Then I told her everything. In the middle of me telling her what Lucas had said, my pager went off.

Grayson's number popped up and the numbers one-one flashed on the screen. I gave the same message back.

CHAPTER EIGHTEEN
SWOON WORTHY
CAMMY

The Spice Girls echoed through the food court. The lunch crowd was heavy today, especially with the special I had suggested to Gus. Buy two tacos and get one free.

I couldn't remember ever being so busy like this, but it was good for business, even if I had to work my ass off. We were even shorthanded and I had to do double shifts. Sometimes I had to cook, and sometimes I was the cashier.

It had been a few days since Grayson and I agreed to be more than friends. The pain in my heart had ceased to exist. Leah had been right. Once I found the one meant for me, nothing else mattered. Leah was over the moon when I told her. Not only had she squealed, but she had thrown in, "I told you so."

It felt strange to cut Lucas off completely as if I never knew him. I supposed it was better so that both of us could heal. Regardless of what Lucas had done, I knew he was hurting, too. He did care for me, though I wasn't sure how deeply he loved me. Not enough, judging from the way he flirted with other girls. And how many times had he cheated behind my back? I didn't want to know. The past was the past.

"I thought the line would never end." Tracy wiped beads of sweat from her forehead.

Gus dropped his shoulders from exhaustion but held a smile as he swiped the damp cloth over the counter. "We need to have a special again. Did you see how long our line was compared to others?"

I tossed my hands up in the air, rolling my eyes. "No. I didn't notice. We were drowning with customers. Next time, make sure to staff appropriately."

Gus shook his hair back and shrugged. "So grouchy. You don't have a boyfriend. Have you lost Grayson's friendship, too?" He placed his hand-held cloth over his heart in devastation when he mentioned Grayson.

As if on cue, a tall, sculpted god with a cap backward on his head swaggered toward me. Girls waved, called out his name in greeting, and tried to get his attention, but his eyes were rooted on me. A lion to his lioness filled with hunger and want.

"Holy shit." Gus fanned his face. "It's too hot in here."

I wasn't sure what Gus had said as I, too, took in Grayson's sexy stride, his dimples deepening and his smile widening the closer he got to me.

"Hi." He planted his hands on the counter.

"Hi." My lips curled wide, my heart and stomach fluttering with joy and nerves.

"You get out at five, right?"

"Yes," I breathed.

"It's almost five. I made it just in time. I have dinner waiting for us back at my place."

I raised my eyebrows. "You cooked for me? Your place?" my voice escaped teasingly.

"I won, remember? I think it's time to pay up."

I recalled that bet over the test when he said the sweetest thing. "You didn't have to do that."

Grayson's eyelashes lowered for only a second to check his watch. "Gus," he called, his eyes still pinned on me as if he was afraid I would disappear.

Gus lightly bumped shoulders with me. "What do you need, Grayson?"

With his eyes never leaving mine, he said with that irresistible grin, "You have no customers. Tell Cams she's free to go."

"But it's not five yet," Gus challenged.

Grayson ever so slowly craned his neck to Gus with lips straight as a pencil. "Cams worked her ass off for you today. Don't dock her pay." He turned to me with that signature Grayson-dimpled grin. "I'm taking my girl home."

Grayson swung over the counter, cradled me in his arms, and took me out with people gawking at us.

CHAPTER NINETEEN
MY SISTER'S GRADUATION
CAMMY

Two Months Later

"Mom. Dad. Casey." I waved at them. Holding Grayson's hand, I led him toward my family in the sea of people. After the introduction and hugs, Casey linked my arm and pulled me to the side.

"He seems like a nice guy, and he's really cute." Her eyes darted to Grayson and back to me.

Grayson was talking away with my parents. He glanced my way, winked, and continued the conversation.

"Yeah. He's wonderful. I'm so lucky he's mine."

"He's lucky to have you, big sis."

I blinked at Casey's words and smiled. "Thank you, little sis. You look beautiful, and I'm so proud of you."

"Thank you. That means a lot to me coming from you. Go find your seats. I have to go now."

Casey gave me a hug and went to be with the other graduates.

"Grayson seems like a great guy. He's good to you?" Mom leaned in to whisper once we were seated.

Mom knew the details of why Lucas and I had broken up. She felt sad for me, but she also told me it was better to know now than later.

"He is, Mom. He's everything I want."

"I'm happy for you." Mom kissed my cheek and stroked my hair.

When the music began, Grayson placed his arm around my shoulder and held my hand with his free hand.

"Thank you." I kissed his lips.

"For what?"

"For being wonderful. For being in my life. For waiting for me. For being my best friend."

Grayson tenderly kissed my forehead. So much love and devotion showed in that kiss. "You're mine and I'm yours." He kissed me again. "Next week, I want to take you to my parents'. They're going to love you."

"Sure. I can't wait."

As he stared into my eyes, his blue eyes like the sky above and his dimples defined, I inhaled a deep breath, feeling my heart expanding, and realized what love truly felt like.

Lucas used to tell me I would always be his baby, but I never believed him, never felt it. But with Grayson...

"You'll always be my baby," I whispered into his ear. It was too soon to say such intimate words, but he made it easy.

Grayson's eyes darkened. "And you'll always be mine. I can't wait to take you home." He planted a kiss, and as he tugged my bottom lip with his teeth, he released an animalistic possessive growl.

Quivering, I took his hand into mine and we watched the ceremony together.

I can't wait for you to read:

WHEN THE WIND CHIMES
Pub date: November 10, 2020

Kaitlyn Summers is heartbroken.

When she receives an invitation to spend Christmas with her family on the Hawaiian island of Kauai, she feels it may be the perfect medicine.

She throws herself into helping her sister's struggling art gallery, even taking a temporary job for extra money by looking after a little girl from her nephew's school. She also begins to paint again, something she's been unable to do since her breakup. It's tempting to stay on Kauai, but she has obligations back in Los Angeles.

Life gets more complicated when circumstances keep putting her close to Leonardo Medici. Not only is he drop-dead gorgeous, he's a local celebrity. But Kaitlyn can't shake the feeling he's hiding something.

Should she believe the rumors that he's romancing half the island's single women?

Or is the random sound of wind chimes when he's close-by a sign that an angel is near and the secret to her happily ever after?

115

International Bestselling, Award-Winning Author Mary Ting writes soulful, spellbinding stories that excite the imagination and captivate readers all over the world. Her books run a wide range of genres: science fiction, fantasy, and swoon worthy stories. Her storytelling talents have won her a devoted legion of fans and garnered critical praise.

Mary was born in Seoul Korea and resides in Southern California with her husband, two children, and two dogs—Mochi and Mocha. She enjoys oil painting and making jewelry. Becoming an author was a way to grieve the death of her beloved grandmother. After realizing she wanted to become a full-time author, she retired from teaching after twenty years.

www.tangledtalesofting.com

Other Books by Mary Ting

Rosewind Books
When The Wind Chimes 11/10/20

From Vesuvian Books
ISAN - International Sensory Assassin Network
Helix (Book 2 of ISAN)
GENES (Book 3 of ISAN)
Jaclyn and the Beanstalk

The Crossroads Saga
Crossroads
Between
Beyond
Eternity
Halo City (Novella)

Descendant Prophecies Series
From Gods
From Deities
From Origins
From Titans

Secret Knights Series
The Angel Knights (Novella)
The Chosen Knights
The Blessed Knights
The Sacred Knights

Watcher Series
Book of Watchers
Book of Enchantresses

Novella Romance
Always Be My Baby